# Infancy

## by Thornton Wilder

A SAMUEL FRENCH ACTING EDITION

SAMUEL FRENCH
FOUNDED 1830

SAMUELFRENCH.COM

## FOR PRODUCTION ENQUIRIES

### UNITED STATES AND CANADA
Info@SamuelFrench.com
1-866-598-8449

### AMATEUR RIGHTS IN THE
### UNITED KINGDOM
Plays@SamuelFrench-London.co.uk
020-7255-4302

Each title is subject to availability from Samuel French, depending
upon country of performance. Please be aware that *INFANCY* may
not be licensed by Samuel French in your territory. Producers should
contact the nearest Samuel French office or licensing partner to verify
availability.

For all enquiries regarding professional productions in the United
Kingdom; Professional and Amateur productions throughout the rest of
Europe; and motion picture, television, and other media rights, please
contact Alan Brodie Representation (Victoria@AlanBrodie.com). Visit
www.thorntonwilder.com/contact for details.

No one shall make any changes in this title for the purpose of production. No part of this book may be reproduced, stored in a retrieval system, or transmitted in any form, by any means, now known or yet to be invented, including mechanical, electronic, photocopying, recording, videotaping, or otherwise, without the prior written permission of the publisher. No one shall upload this title, or part of this title, to any social media websites.

## MUSIC USE NOTE

Licensees are solely responsible for obtaining formal written permission from copyright owners to use copyrighted music in the performance of this play and are strongly cautioned to do so. If no such permission is obtained by the licensee, then the licensee must use only original music that the licensee owns and controls. Licensees are solely responsible and liable for all music clearances and shall indemnify the copyright owners of the play and their licensing agent, Samuel French, against any costs, expenses, losses and liabilities arising from the use of music by licensees. Please contact the appropriate music licensing authority in your territory for the rights to any incidental music.

## IMPORTANT BILLING AND CREDIT REQUIREMENTS

All producers of *INFANCY* must give credit to the author of the play in all programs distributed in connection with performances of the play, and in all instances in which the title of the play appears for the purposes of advertising, publicizing or otherwise exploiting the play and/or a production. The name of the author must appear on a separate line on which no other name appears, immediately following the title and must appear in size of type not less than fifty percent of the size of the title type.

This play may be performed only in its entirety. No permission can be granted for cuttings, readings or any use of parts of the play for any purpose whatsoever without the express written permission of the Wilder Family LLC. Absolutely *no* changes can be made to the text.

# FOREWORD TO *INFANCY*

## THE FIRST PLAY IN THORNTON WILDER'S
### *AGES OF MAN* ONE-ACT PLAY CYCLE

From the time he began dreaming up plays as a boy Thornton Wilder's vision of the theater transcended conventional boundaries, and to the end of his life his vision continually evolved and expanded. In 1956, he began work on what grew into an extravagantly ambitious project: two cycles of seven one-act plays based on the Deadly Sins and the Ages of Man. *Infancy* is the first play in Wilder's series on the Ages of Man.

In what would prove to be his final dramatic works, Wilder sought not only to explore the theatrical possibilities inherent in the Sins and Ages, but (as he phrased it in his private journal on Christmas Day 1960) to "offer each play in the series as representing, also, a different mode of playwriting: Grand Guignol, Chekhov, Noh play, etc., etc." In short, he envisioned nothing less than a tour de force of dramatic theme and form encapsulated in the economy and intensity of the one-act play.

Wilder did not complete the challenge he set for himself, but he came close. The surviving work enriches his dramatic legacy and deserves to be remembered as more than a footnote to his lifelong conviction (written soon after *Our Town* opened on Broadway in 1938): "The theater offers to imaginative narration its highest possibilities."

### THE SINS AND AGES THEN AND NOW

A brief overview of the history of these plays will help readers place them in Wilder's career as a dramatist. Two Sins, *Bernice* (Pride) and *The Wreck on the 5:25* (Sloth), premiered in English at a special event in Berlin in 1957 (with Wilder performing in *Bernice*). For reasons that have never been clear, for he enjoyed the experience and felt that plays did well, he withdrew them. That same year a third Sin, *The Drunken Sisters* (Gluttony), written as the satyr play for Wilder's full length drama, *The Alcestiad*, proved successful in its premiere on the stage of Zürich's fabled Schauspielhaus.

Five years passed before the continuation of his ambitious scheme appeared on a stage in the United States. In January 1962, two new Ages, *Infancy* and *Childhood*, and a new Sin, *Someone From Assisi* (Lust), opened at Circle in the Square, then located off-Broadway on Bleecker Street, to the reported largest pre-opening advanced sale in that stage's then 11- year history. Billed as "Plays for Bleecker Street," the show of ran for 349 performances.

Then silence. After "Plays for Bleecker Street" closed, no more Sins or Ages appeared. When Thornton Wilder died in 1975 the public record of his 14-play scheme contained only four plays – two Ages (*Infancy* and *Childhood*) and two Sins (Lust and Gluttony).

Today, eleven of Wilder's Sins and Ages are available for production: a completed cycle of the seven Deadly Sins and four of seven Ages of Man. The source of the seven "new" plays is no secret. The missing pieces were found in Thornton Wilder's archives at Yale[1]. From this source, starting in 1995, his literary executor and family released the two plays withdrawn in 1957, *Cement Hands* (Avarice), and four additional titles (*Youth, The Rivers Under the Earth* [Middle Age][2], *A Ringing of Doorbells* [Envy] and *In Shakespeare and the Bible* [Wrath]) recovered and completed by the actor, director and friend of Wilder's, F.J. O'Neil. (Mr. O'Neil's valuable notes on the origin of each of these missing links follow the text of each play.)

The public reception of Thornton Wilder's long lost and new plays was gratifying. *The Wreck on the 5:25* was selected as one of the Best American Short Plays of 1994-95. In 1997, the Centenary of the playwright's birth, Kevin Kline starred in a premiere reading in New York of *Cement Hands*, and the works recovered by Mr. O'Neil served as the centerpieces of Actors Theatre of Louisville's 13th Annual Brown-Forman Classics in Context Festival.   Finally, as the capstone to the Centenary celebration, TCG Press in 1997 published the 11 Sins and Ages in Volume I of *The Collected Short Plays of Thornton Wilder.*

---

[1] No additional one-acts remain to be discovered in Thornton Wilder's archives at Yale.

[2] We believe Wilder intended *The Rivers Under the Earth* to represent Middle Age.

Wilder never followed conventional theatrical practice. As a young writer in his "Classic One Act Plays" of 1931, he swept away scenery and played provocative games with time and place. In the Sins and Ages, his farewell as a playwright, he is no less adventurous by way of settings, techniques, stage-craft and themes. One artistic trend of the day especially "fired his imagination" where these plays are concerned: his passionate belief in the value of the arena stage. "The boxed set play," he wrote in 1961, "encourages the anecdote...The unencumbered stage encourages the truth in everyone." Wilder felt so strongly that audiences should be seated as close to the actors as possible that Samuel French, for several years, was only permitted to license these plays to companies agreeing to perform them on a three-sided thrust or arena stage.

***

As part of its celebration of Wilder's one-act plays, Samuel French and the Wilder family take great pleasure in issuing new acting editions for the Sins and Ages long in print and, for the first time, acting editions of the seven new Wilder works. We invite those performing or teaching these plays to visit www.thorntonwilder.com for additional information.

– *Tappan Wilder,*
Literary Executor for Thornton Wilder

## CHARACTERS

**OFFICER AVONZINO**

**MISS MILLIE WILCHICK** – a nursemaid

**TOMMY** – a baby in her care

**MRS. BOKER**

**MOE** – Mrs. Boker's baby boy

## SETTING

Central Park in New York City. The 1920s.

*(One or more large park benches. Some low stools at the edges of the stage indicate bushes.)*

*(Enter* **OFFICER AVONZINO**, *a policeman from the Keystone comic movies with a waterfall mustache, thick black eyebrows and a large silver star. Swinging his billy club jauntily, he shades his eyes and peers down the paths for trouble. Reassured, he extracts a small memorandum book from an inner pocket of his jacket and reads:)*

AVONZINO. "Wednesday, April 26..." Right. "Centra' Park, Patrol Section Eleven, West, Middle." Right! "Lieutenant T. T. Avonzino." Correct. Like Tomaso Tancredo Avonzino. "Eight to twelve; two to six. Special Orders: Suspect – mad dog, black with white spots. Suspect – old gentleman, silk hat, pinches nurses." *(reflects)* Pinch babies okay; pinch nurses, nuisance. *(puts the book away, strolls, then takes it out again for further instructions)* Probable weather: late morning, precipitation – precipitation like rain. *(strolls)* Seven to eight-thirty, no nuisances. Millionaires on horses; horses on millionaires. Young gents running in underwear; old gents running in underwear. *(reflects)* Running in underwear, okay; *walking* in underwear, nuisance. Eight-thirty to nine-thirty, everybody late for working, rush-rush, no time for nuisances. Nine-thirty to twelve, babies. One thousand babies with ladies. Nuisances plenty: old gents poisoning pigeons; ladies stealing baby carriages. Nuisances in bushes: young gents and young girls taking liberties. *(hotly)* Why can't they do their nuisances at home? That's what homes are for: to do your nuisances in. *(He shields his eyes and peers toward the actors' entrance at the back of the stage; emotionally.)* Here she comes! Miss'a Wilchick! *Baby!* – prize baby of Centra' Park.

AVONZINO. *(cont.) (He extracts a handbook from another pocket of his jacket.)* "Policeman's Guide. Lesson Six: Heart Attacks and Convulsions." No. No. "Lesson Sixteen: Frostbite." No! "Lesson Eleven:…" Ha! "An officer exchanges no personal remarks wid de public." Crazy! *(in dreamy ecstasy)* Oh, personal re-marks. It's personal remarks dat make-a de world go round; dat make-a de birds sing. *(indignantly)* Nobody, *nobody* wid flesh and blood can live widout'a personal re-marks. Ha! She comes!… *(He steals off by the aisle through the audience.)*

*(Enter from the back* **MISS MILLIE WILCHICK**, *pushing Tommy's baby carriage.* **TOMMY**, *now invisible in the carriage, is to be played by a full-grown man.* **MILLIE** *brings the carriage to rest by a bench. She peers up the various paths in search of* **OFFICER AVONZINO**. *Disappointed, she prepares to make herself comfortable. From the foot of the carriage she brings out a box of chocolates, another of marshmallows, and a novel. Before sitting down she talks into the carriage.)*

MILLIE. …lil sweet lovums. Miss Millie's lil lover, aren't you? Yes, you are. I could squeeze lil Tommy to death, yes. I could. Kiss-kiss-kiss, yes, I could. *(again peering down the paths)* Don't know where Mr. Policerman is! Big handsome Officer Avonzino. He take care of Miss Millie and lil lover-boy Tommy…Hmm…Maybe he come by and by. *(She sits on the bench and selects a candy.)* … Peppermint…strawb'ry?…Well, and a marshmallow. *(She opens the novel at the first page and reads with great deliberation.)* "Doris was not strictly beautiful, but when she passed, men's heads turned to gaze at her with pleasure. Doris was not strictly beautiful, but…" *(a squeal of joy)* Oh, they *don't* write like that any more!! Oh, I'm going to enjoy this book. Let's see how it ends. First, there must be one of those chawclut cream centers. *(She turns to the last page of the novel.)* "He drew her to him, pressing his lips on hers. 'Forever,' he said. Doris closed her eyes. 'Forever,' she said. The end."

*(delighted cry)* They don't write like that any more. "For e…e…ever." Could I say "forever," if his lips… "e-e-v"…were pressed on mine? *(She closes her eyes and experiments.)* …e…ver…for…e…Yes, I guess it could be done. *(She starts dreaming.)* Oh, I *know* I could write a novel. *(She dreams.)*

*(Slowly* **TOMMY***'s hands can be seen gripping the side of his carriage. With great effort he pulls himself up until his head appears. He is wearing a lace-trimmed cap.)*

**TOMMY.** Fur…evvah…Do-rus…nah…strigly bootoody… *(fretfully)* I can't say it…boody-fill…Why don't they teach me to say it? I want to LEARN and they won't teach me. Do-rua nah stackly…boody…Fur evvah… *(near to wailing)* Time's going by. I'm getting owe-uld. And nobody is showing me *anything.* I wanta make a house. I wanta make a house. I wanta make a bay-beee. Nobody show-ow-ow-s me how-ta.

**MILLIE.** *(waking up)* Tommy! What are you crying about? Has 'a got a little stummyache? Has 'a got a foot caught? No. *(leaning over him, suddenly severe)* Has Tommy wet his bed?!! No. No. Then's what's a matter?

**TOMMY.** Wanta make a house!

**MILLIE.** Wants to be petted, yes.

**TOMMY.** *(violently)* Wanta make a baybeee!

**MILLIE.** Miss Millie's lil lover wants a little attention.

**TOMMY.** *(fortissimo)* Chawclut. Chawclut. Wanta eat what you're eating. Wanta eat what you smell of…chawclut.

**MILLIE.** Now don't you climb up. You'll fall out. It's terrible the way you're growing.

**TOMMY.** Put me on the ground. I wanta learn to walk. I wanta walk. I wanta walk. I wanta find things to *eat.*

**MILLIE.** *(sternly)* Now Miss Millie's going to spank you. Crying for nothing. You ought to be ashamed of yourself.

*(She stands joggling the baby carriage with one hand and holding the opened novel with the other.)*

MILLIE. *(cont.)* "This little pig went to *mar-ket.*" There! "This little pig..." shhshh – shh! "Doris was not strictly beautiful, but..." Oh, I read that. "This little pig stayed at home." *(She looks into the carriage with great relief.)* God be praised in His glory, babies get tired soon...Asleep. *(She walks across the stage; then suddenly stops.)* I don't know what I'm going to do. My life is hell. Here I am, a good-looking girl almost thirty and *nothing ever happens.* Everybody's living, except me. Everybody's happy, except ME!! *(She returns, sobbing blindly to the baby carriage.)* Those silly novels – I hate them – just gab-gab-gab. Now I'm crying so I can't see which is pineapple. *(She chances to look in the direction of the aisle through the audience.)* Oh, my God, there comes Officer Avonzino. *(She clasps her hands in fervent prayer.)* Oh, my God, help a girl! If you ever helped a girl, help her now!

*(She rapidly hides novel and candy under* TOMMY*'s blankets, and takes out another book. She arranges herself at one end of the bench and pretends to fall into a reverie.)*

*(Enter* OFFICER AVONZINO *through the audience. He steals behind* MILLIE *and puts his hands over her eyes. The following passage is very rapid.)*

AVONZINO. You've got one guessing coming to you! *Who* is in Centra' Park? Maybe who?

MILLIE. Oh, I don't know. I really don't.

AVONZINO. You've got two guessings. Maybe the mayor of Newa-York, maybe him, you think? Now you got one guessing. Maybe T. T. Avonzino – like somebody you know, somebody you seen before.

MILLIE. Oh! Officer Avonzino!!

*(He leaps on the bench beside her. She is kept busy removing his hands from her knees.)*

AVONZINO. Somebody you know. Somebody you seen before.

MILLIE. Officer, you must behave. You really must behave.

AVONZINO. Action! I believe is a action! Personal remarks and da action.

(**TOMMY** *has raised himself and is staring enormous-eyed and with great disapproval at these goings-on.*)

TOMMY. *(loudly)* Ya! Ya! Ya! Ya! Ya!

(**OFFICER AVONZINO** *is thunderstruck. He jumps up as though caught out of order by his superior. He stands behind the bench adjusting his tie and coat and star.*)

MILLIE. Why, what's the matter, Mr. Avonzino?

AVONZINO. *(low and terse)* Him. Looka at him. Looka at him, looking.

TOMMY. Ya. Ya. Ya.

MILLIE. Go to sleep, Tommy. Just nice policerman. Tommy's friend. Go to sleep.

TOMMY. *(one last warning, emphatically)* Ya!

*(He disappears.)*

MILLIE. But, Officer, he's just a *baby*. He doesn't understand one little thing.

AVONZINO. *(blazing, but under his breath)* Oh no, oh no, oh no, oh no – he got thoughts. Turn-a de carriage around. I no wanta see that face.

MILLIE. *(turning the carriage)* I'm surprised at you. He's just a dear little baby. A dear little…animal.

AVONZINO. Miss Wilchick, I see one thousand babies a day. They got *ideas*.

MILLIE. *(laughing girlishly)* Why, Mr. Avonzino, you're like the author of this book I've been reading. – Dr. Kennick. He says babies are regular geniuses in their first fourteen months. He says: you know why babies sleep all the time? Because they're learning all the time, they get tired by learning. Geniuses, he says, imagine!

AVONZINO. *What* he say?

MILLIE. They learn more than they'll ever learn again. And faster. Like hands and feet; and to focus your eyes. And like walking and talking. He says their brains are exploding with power.

AVONZINO. What he say?

MILLIE. Well – after about a year they stop being geniuses. Dr. Kennick says the reason why we aren't geniuses is that we weren't brought up right: we were stopped.

AVONZINO. That's a right. He gotta the right idea. Miss Wilchick, I see one thousand babies a day. And what I say is: stop 'em. That's your business, Miss Wilchick; that's my business. There's too many ingeniouses in Centra' Park right now: stop 'em.

(TOMMY *begins to howl.* AVONZINO *points at him with his billy club.*)

What did I tell you? They all understand English. North' a Eighth Street they all understand English.

MILLIE. *(leaning over Tommy's carriage)* There, there. Nice policerman don't mean *one* word of it.

AVONZINO. *(Looking at the actors' entrance; they are both shouting to be heard.)* Here comes another brains. I go now.

MILLIE. Oh, that must be Mrs. Boker – I'm so sorry this happened, Mr. Avonzino.

AVONZINO. I see you later, maybe – when you get permission from the professor – permission in writing, Miss Wilchick. *(He goes out through the audience.)*

(*Enter* MRS. BOKER *pushing Moe's carriage.* MOE *starts crying in sympathy with* TOMMY. *Both women shout.*)

MRS. BOKER. What's the matter with Tommy – good morning – on such a fine day?

MILLIE. *(leaning over* TOMMY*)* What's a matter?

TOMMY. CHAWCLUT!! STRAWB'RY!! I'm hungreee.

MILLIE. Really, I don't know what ails the child.

MRS. BOKER. *(leaning over Moe's carriage; beginning loud but gradually lowering her voice as both babies cease howling)* …K…L…M…N…O…P…Q…R…S…T… Have you ever noticed, Miss Wilchick, that babies get quiet when you say the alphabet to them? …W…X…Y…A…B… C…D… I don't understand it. Moe is mad about the alphabet. Same way with the multiplication table.

**MRS. BOKER.** *(cont.)* *(to* **MOE,** *who is now silent)* Three times five are fifteen. Three times six are eighteen. When my husband has to keep Moe quiet: the multiplication table! Never fails! My husband calls him Isaac Newton. – Seven times five are thirty-five. Eight times five are forty. Never fails.

**MILLIE.** *(intimidated)* Really?

**MRS. BOKER.** *(pointing to the silent carriages)* Well, look for yourself! Isn't silence grand? *(She sits on a bench and starts taking food out of* **MOE** *'s carriage.)* Now, dear, have some potato chips. Or pretzels. What do you like?

**MILLIE.** Well, you have some of my marshmallows and candy.

**MRS. BOKER.** Marshmallows! Oh, I know I shouldn't! – Have you noticed that being around babies makes you think of eating all the time? I don't know why that is. *(pushing* **MILLIE** *in raucous enjoyment of the joke)* Like, being with babies makes us like babies. And you know what *they* think about!!

**MILLIE.** *(convulsed)* Oh, Mrs. Boker, what will you say next! – How is Moe, Mrs. Boker?

**MRS. BOKER.** *(her mouth full)* How *is* he!! Sometimes I wish he'd be sick for *one* day – just to give me a present. *(lowering her voice)* I don't have to tell you what life with a baby is: *(looking around circumspectly)* It's *war – one long war.* – Excuse me, I can't talk while he's listening. *(She rises and wheels* **MOE** *'s carriage to a distance; returning, she continues in a lowered voice.)* My husband believes that Moe understands every word we say.

**MILLIE.** Mrs. Boker!

**MRS. BOKER.** I don't know what to believe, but one thing I do know: that baby lies on the floor and listens to every word we say. At first my husband took to spelling out words, you know – but Albert Einstein, there – in two weeks he got them all. He would *look* at my husband, *look* at him with those big eyes! And then my husband took to talking in Yiddish – see what I mean? – but no! In two weeks Albert Einstein got Yiddish.

**MILLIE.** But, Mrs. Boker!! It's just a baby! He don't under-stand *one word*.

**MRS. BOKER.** *You* know that. *I* know that. But *(pointing to the carriage)* does *he* know that? It's driving my husband crazy. "Turn it in and get a dog," he says. "I didn't ask for no prodigy," he says. "All I wanted was a baby – " *(lowering her voice)* Of course, most of the time my husband worships Moe...only...only we don't know what to do with him, as you might say.

**MILLIE.** Oh, you imagine it, Mrs. Boker!

**MRS. BOKER.** Listen to me! – Have some of these pret-zels; they'll be good after those sweets. Listen to me, Junior's at the crawling stage. He does fifty miles a day. My husband calls him Christopher Columbus. – My husband's stepped on him five times.

**MILLIE.** Mrs. Boker! You've got a playpen, haven't you?

**MRS. BOKER.** PLAYPEN!! He's broke two, hasn't he? We can't afford to buy no lion's cage, Miss Wilchick – besides, Macy's don't sell them. Now listen to me: Christopher Columbus follows us wherever we go, see? When I get supper – there he is! He could make a gefilte fish tomorrow. That child – mad about the bathroom! Know what I mean? My husband says he has a "something" mind – you know: d. i. r. t. y.

**MILLIE.** Mrs. Boker.

**MRS. BOKER.** Sometimes I wish I had a girl – only it'd be just my luck to get one of those Joans of Arcs.
   *(MOE starts to howl.)*
   There he goes! Like I said: understands *every* word we say. Now watch this: *(She leans over MOE's carriage, holding a handkerchief before her mouth.)* You mustn't let them smell what you've been eating, *or else* – Listen, Moe, like I was telling you: New York City is divided into five boroughs. There's the Bronx, Moe, and Brooklyn and Queens – *(MOE quiets almost at once.)*
   See how it works? – Richmond and Manhattan. – It's crazy, I know, but what can I do about that? – Yes, Manhattan; the largest, like I told you, is Manhattan. Yes, Manhattan.

*(She looks in the carriage. Silence.)* Isn't it a blessing that they get tired so soon? He's exhausted by the boroughs already.

**MILLIE.** But he doesn't understand a word of it!!

**MRS. BOKER.** What has understanding got to do with it, Miss Wilchick? I don't understand the telephone, but I *telephone.*

*(**TOMMY** has raised his head and is listening big-eyed.)*

**TOMMY.** N'Yak Citee divi fife burrs. Manha...Manha...Manha... *(He starts crying with frustration.)* I can't *say* it. I can't *say* it.

**MRS. BOKER.** Now yours is getting excited.

**TOMMY.** I can't talk and nobody'll teach me. I can't talk...

**MRS. BOKER.** *(loud)* Go over and put him to sleep.

**MILLIE.** *(loud)* But I don't know the boroughs. Please, Mrs. Boker, just once, you show me.

**MRS. BOKER.** I'll try something else. Watch this! Listen, Tommy, are you listening? "I pledge legions to my flag and to the republic in which it stands." You were a girl scout, weren't you? "Something something invisible with liberty and justice for all."

*(**TOMMY** has fallen silent.)*

"I pledge legions to my flag..."

**MILLIE.** *(awed)* Will anything work?

**MRS. BOKER.** *(lowering her voice)* They don't like those lullabies and "This little pig went to market." See, they like it *serious.* There's nothing in the world so serious like a baby. – Well, now we got a little quiet again.

**MILLIE.** Mrs. Boker, can I ask you a question about Moe?... Take one of these; it's pineapple inside...Is Moe, like they say, housebroken?

**MRS. BOKER.** Moe?! Gracious sakes! Moe makes a great show of it. I guess there isn't a thing in the world that interests Moe like going to his potty. *(She laughs.)* When he wants to make us a present: *off* he goes! When he's angry at us…oh, no! He plays it like these violinists play their violin…which reminds me!… *(looking about her speculatively)* Do you suppose…I could just…slip behind these bushes a minute?…is that police officer around?

**MILLIE.** Well-ah…Officer Avonzino is awfully particular about nuisances, what he calls nuisances. Maybe you could go over to the avenue there – there's a branch library…

**MRS. BOKER.** Will you be an angel and watch Moe for me? If he starts to cry, give him the days of the week and the months of the year. He *loves* them. – Now where's this library?

**MILLIE.** Why, the Museum of National History's right over there.

**MRS. BOKER.** *(scream of pleasure)* Museum of Natural History!! How could I have forgotten that! Just full of animals. Of *course*! I won't be a minute, dear!…

*(They exchange good-byes.* **MRS. BOKER** *goes out.* **MILLIE** *eyes Moe's carriage apprehensively, then seats herself and resumes her novel at the last page.)*

**MILLIE.** "Roger came into the room. His fine strong face still bore the marks of the suffering he had experienced." Oh! I imagine his wife died. Isn't that wonderful! He's *free*! "He drew her to him, pressing his lips on hers. 'Forever,' he said." Oh! "For-ever."

*(In a moment, she is asleep.)*

*(**TOMMY** pulls himself up and stares at **MOE**'s carriage.)*

**TOMMY.** Moe!…Moe!

**MOE.** *(surging up furiously)* Don't make noises at me! Don't look at me! Don't do anything. *(telephone business, swiftly)* Hello, g'bye! *(He disappears.)*

**TOMMY.** Moe!…Moe!…Talk to me something!…Moe, why are you that way at me?

**MOE.** *(surging up again, glaring)* My daddy says I'm stupid. He says, "Stupid, come here!" He says, "All right, stupid, fall down!" I don't want to talk. I don't want to look. G'bye!

*(He disappears.)*

**TOMMY.** What does "stupid" mean?

**MOE.** *(invisible)* I won't tell. *(surging up, showing his fingers; a rapid-fire jumble)* Do you know what these are? Sometimes you call them fingers; sometimes you call them piggies. One, two, six, five, four, two, ten. This little piggie stayed at home, I don't know why that is. Do you know what you do when the loud bell rings? You do this: *(telephone business)* "Hello...jugga...jugga... jugga," and when you don't like it any more you say, "G'bye!" Maybe I am stupid. – But that's because MY MOUTH HURTS ALL THE TIME and they don't give me enough to eat and I'm hungry all the time and that's the end of it, that's the end of it.

*(He disappears.)*

**TOMMY.** Moe, tell me some more things.

**MOE.** *(surging up again)* "Stupid, come here!" "Stupid, get your goddamn tail out of here!" *(shaking his carriage)* I hate him. I hate him. But I watch him and I learn. *You see*: I learn. And when I get to walk I'm going to do something so that he won't *be* any more. He'll be away – away where people can walk on him. – Don't you hate your father?

**TOMMY.** Well...I don't see him much. Like, once a year.

**MOE.** You mean: once a day.

**TOMMY.** Moe, what does "year" mean?

**MOE.** Year is when it's cold.

**TOMMY.** *(brightening)* Yes, I know.

**MOE.** Sometimes he holds out his hands and says: "How's the little fella? How's the little champ?" And I give him a look! I wasn't born yesterday. He hasn't got anything to sell to me.

**TOMMY.** Moe – where's your mommy? *(silence)* Moe, she's not here. Where's your mommy? You don't hate your mommy, do you?

MOE. *(turning his face sideways, cold and proud)* I don't care about her. She's always away. She goes away for years. She laughs at me...with that *man*. He says: "All right, fall down, stupid," and she laughs. I try to talk to her and she goes away all the time and does, "Hello – jugga – jugga-jugga-goo-bye!" If she don't care about me any more, I don't care about her any more. Goo-bye! *(silence)*

TOMMY. Say some more, Moe, say some more things.

MOE. *(low and intense)* Maybe I am stupid. Maybe I'll never be able to walk or make talk. Maybe they didn't give me good feet or a good mouth. – You know what I think? I think they don't want us to walk and to get good and get better. They want us to *stop*. That's what I think. *(His voice has risen to a hysterical wail.)* Goddam! Hell! *(He starts throwing cloth elephants and giraffes out of the carriage.)* I'm not going to try. Nobody wants to help me and lots of time is passing and I'm not getting bigger, and...and... *(anticlimax)* I'm sleepeee... *(He continues to whimper.)*

*(*MILLIE *wakes up. She goes gingerly to* MOE*'s carriage and joggles it.)*

MILLIE. Moe! What's the matter, Moe? "Rockabye, baby, in the treetop – "

*(*MOE *wails more loudly.)*

Oh, goodness, gracious me. *(in desperation)* Moe! Do you know that *that* street is called Central Park West? And then there's Columbus Avenue? And then there's Amsterdam Avenue? And then there's Broadway?

*(*MOE *has hushed.)*

And then there's West End Avenue. *(She can hardly believe her luck; she whispers:)* And then there's Riverside Drive. *(She peers into the carriage a long time, then tiptoes to the other end of the stage; with clenched fists.)* I hate babies. *(toward* TOMMY*)* I hate you – sticking your crazy face into my business – frightening Officer Avonzino, the only man I've talked to in six months. I hate you – always butting in. I have a right to my own life, haven't I? *My own life!* I'm sick to death of squalling, smelling, gawking babies...I'd be a stenographer only I don't know anything; nobody ever taught me anything... "Manhattan, the Bronx" – what do I care what keeps you quiet? You can yell your heads off for all I care! I don't know why nature didn't make it so that people came into the world already grown-up – instead of a dozen and more years of screaming and diapers and falling down and breaking everything... and asking questions! "What's that?" "Why-y-y?" "Why-y-y?"...Officer Avonzino will never come back, that's certain!...Oh, what do I care? You're going to grow up to be men – nasty, selfish men. You're all alike.

*(Drying her eyes, she picks up her novel from* **TOMMY***'s carriage and strolls off the stage at the back.)*

*(**MOE***'s head, now solemn and resolute, rises slowly.)*

**MOE.** Tommy!...Tommy!

**TOMMY.** *(appearing)* I'm tired.

**MOE.** You know what I'm going to do, do you?

**TOMMY.** No – what, Moe?

**MOE.** I'm just going to lie still.

**TOMMY.** What do you mean, Moe?

**MOE.** I'll shut my eyes and do nothing. I won't eat. I'll just go away-away. Like I want Daddy to do.

**TOMMY.** *(alarm)* No, Moe! Don't go where people can walk on you!

**MOE.** Well, I *will*...You know what I think? I think people aren't SERIOUS about us. "Little piggie went to market, cradle will fall, Manhattan, the Bronx" – that's not serious. They don't want us to get better.

**TOMMY.** *Maybe* they do.

**MOE.** Old people are only interested in old people. Like kiss-kiss-kiss; that's all they do; that's all they think about.

**TOMMY.** *(eagerly)* Ye-e-es! Miss'a Millie, all the time, kiss-kiss-kiss, but she don't mean me; she means the policerman.

**MOE.** We're in the way, see? We're too little, that's how. I don't want to be a man – it's too hard!

*(He disappears.)*

**TOMMY.** *(with increasing alarm)* Moe!…Moe!…Don't stop talking, Moe!…MOE!

*(MILLIE returns hastily.)*

**MILLIE.** Now what's the matter with you? I'll spank you. Always crying and making a baby of yourself.

**TOMMY.** *(at the same time; frantic)* Moe's going away-away. He's not going to eat any more. Go look at Moe…*Do* something. *Do* something!

**MILLIE.** What is the matter with you? Why can't you be quiet like Moe? *(She goes and looks in MOE's carriage and is terrified by what she sees.)* Help!…Hellllp! The baby's turned purple! Moe! Have you swallowed something? – *(She dashes to the audience exit.)* Officer Avonzino! Officer! Hellllp! – Oh, they'll kill me. What'll I do?

*(OFFICER AVONZINO rushes in from the audience.)*

**AVONZINO.** What'a matter, Miss Wilchick; you gone crazy today?

**MILLIE.** *(gasping)* …look…he's turned black, Officer Avonzino…His mother's over at the museum. Oh…I don't know what to do.

*(OFFICER AVONZINO, efficient but unhurried, opens his tunic and takes out his handbook. He hunts for the correct page.)*

**AVONZINO.** First, don't scream, Miss Wilchick. Nobody scream. Babies die every day. Always new babies. Nothing to scream about…Babies turn black – so! Babies turn blue, black, purple, all the time. Hmph "Turn baby over, lift middle…" *(He does these things.)* "Water…" *(to MILLIE)* Go to nurses over there…twenty nurses…Bring back some ippycack.

**MILLIE.** Oh, Officer…help me. I'm fainting.

**AVONZINO.** *(furious)* Faintings on *Sundays* – not workdays, Miss Wilchick.

**MILLIE.** *(hand to head)* Oh…oh…

> *(***OFFICER AVONZINO*** *catches her just in time and drapes her over the bench like a puppet.)*

**AVONZINO.** "Lesson Thirty-Two: Let Mother Die. Save Baby." I get water. *(He dashes off.)*

> *(***TOMMY*** *raises his head.)*

**TOMMY.** Moe! Don't be black. Don't be black. You're going to walk soon. And by and by you can go to school. And even if they don't teach you good, you can kind of teach yourself.

> *(***MOE*** *is sobbing.)*

Moe, what's that noise you're making? Make a crying like a baby, Moe. – Soon you can be big and shave. And be a policerman. And you can make kiss-kiss-kiss…and make babies. And, Moe –

**MOE.** *(appearing)* Don't talk to me. I'm tired. I'm tired.

**TOMMY.** And you can show your babies how to walk and talk.

**MOE.** *(yawning)* I'm…tire'… *(He sinks back.)*

**TOMMY.** *(yawning)* I'm tired, tooooo. *(He sinks back.)*

> *(***OFFICER AVONZINO*** *returns with a child's pail of water. He leans over* ***MOE.****)*

**AVONZINO.** *(astonished)* What'a matter with you!! You all red again. You not sick. Goddamn! Tricks. Babies always doing tricks. *(shakes* ***MILLIE****)* Miss Wilchick! Wake up! Falsa alarm. Baby's okay.

**MILLIE.** *(coming to, dreamily)* Oh, Officer… *(extending her arms amorously)* Oh you're so…handsome…Officer…

**AVONZINO.** *(sternly)* "Lesson Eleven: No Personal Remarks with Public." *(shouts)* It's going to rain: better take George Washington home…and Dr. Einstein, too.

**MILLIE.** Oh! How *is* the Boker baby?

**AVONZINO.** Boker baby's a great actor. Dies every performance. Thousands cheer.

**MILLIE.** *(pushes* **TOMMY** *toward exit)* Oh, I can't go until Mrs. Boker comes back.

*(peers out)* – Oh, there she comes, running. See her?

**AVONZINO.** You *go*. I take care of baby til a'momma comes.

*(At exit* **MILLIE** *turns for a heartfelt farewell; he points billy stick and commands her.)*

Go *faint*, Miss Wilchick!

*(She goes out.* **OFFICER AVONZINO** *addresses* **MOE.***)*

I'd like to make your damn bottom red. I know you. All you babies want the whole world. Well, I tell you, you've got a long hard road before you. Pretty soon you'll find that you can cry all you want and turn every color there is – and nobody'll pay *no* attention at all. Your best days are over; you've had'm. From now on it's all up to you – George Washington, or whatever your name is.

*(enter* **MRS. BOKER***, breathless)*

**MRS. BOKER.** Oh!!

**AVONZINO.** I sent Miss Wilchick home. *(pointing toward rain)* You better start off yourself.

**MRS. BOKER.** *(pushing the carriage to the exit)* Has everything been all right, Officer?

**AVONZINO.** Just fine, lady, just fine. Like usual: babies acting like growed-ups; growed-ups acting like babies.

**MRS. BOKER.** Thank you, Officer.

*(She goes out.)*

*(***OFFICER AVONZINO***, shading his eyes, peers down the aisle through the audience. Suddenly he sees something that outrages him. Like a Keystone cop he does a double take and starts running through the audience, shouting.)*

**AVONZINO.** Hey there!! You leave that baby carriage alone! Don't you know what's inside them baby carriages?...

**End of Play**

THORNTON WILDER (1897-1975) was an accomplished novelist and playwright whose works explore the connection between the commonplace and the cosmic dimensions of human experience. He won three Pulitzer Prizes: for his novel *The Bridge of San Luis Rey*, and two plays, *Our Town* and *The Skin of Our Teeth*. Wilder's farce, *The Matchmaker*, was adapted as the musical *Hello, Dolly!* He also enjoyed enormous success as a translator, adaptor, actor, librettist and lecturer/teacher. Wilder's many honors include the Gold Medal for Fiction from the American Academy of Arts and Letters and the Presidential Medal of Freedom. Penelope Niven's definitive biography, *Thornton Wilder: A Life*, was published in October 2012. For more information, please visit www.thorntonwilder.com.

# Also by
# Thornton Wilder

**The Alcestiad**
**The Beaux' Stratagem (with Ken Ludwig)**
**The Matchmaker**
**Our Town**
**The Skin of Our Teeth**

**Thornton Wilder One Act Series: The Ages of Man**
**Infancy**
**Childhood**
**Youth**
**The Rivers Under the Earth**

**Thornton Wilder One Act Series: The Seven Deadly Sins**
**The Drunken Sisters**
**Bernice**
**The Wreck on the 5:25**
**A Ringing of Doorbells**
**In Shakespeare and the Bible**
**Someone From Assisi**
**Cement Hands**

**Thornton Wilder One Act Series: Wilder's Classic One Acts**
**The Long Christmas Dinner**
**Queens of France**
**Pullman Car Hiawatha**
**Love and How to Cure It**
**Such Things Only Happen in Books**
**The Happy Journey to Trenton and Camden**

www.thorntonwilder.com